THE POETRY WORLD OF JOHN AGARD

ILLUSTRATED BY SHIRLEY HOTTIER

For my mother, Anna de Souza, who grounded me in the circle of her down to earth Creole. For Grace, my soul mate and poet wife, for sharing in the circle. For daughters Lesley, Yansan, Kalera, Grandson Marcus for carrying on the circle. The self-empowering circle of the word. — JA

To my grand-father Louis Raoul Clain (1927-1964) and to all the beautiful souls of my Creole family — SH

ACKNOWLEDGEMENTS

To Janetta Otter-Barry, my great thanks for pursuing and believing in this book. Also, to Charlotte Hacking for her great editorial care, patience and an inspiring push to bring the book to realisation and to Shirley Hottier, whom I have never met, but would like to thank for the wonderful visual empathy in her illustrations.

Text copyright © John Agard 1983, 1986, 1990, 1994, 1996, 2000, 2001, 2025
Introduction copyright © Darren Chetty 2025
Illustrations copyright © Shirley Hottier 2025

The right of John Agard and Shirley Hottier to be identified as the author and illustrator of this work has been asserted by them in accordance with the Copyright, Designs and Patents Act, 1988 (United Kingdom).

First published in Great Britain and in the USA in 2025 by
Otter-Barry Books, Little Orchard, Burley Gate, Herefordshire, HR1 3QS
info@otterbarrybooks.com
www.otterbarrybooks.com

A catalogue record for this book is available from the British Library.

ISBN 978-1-915659-47-7

Illustrated digitally

Set in Dapifer

Printed in China

9 8 7 6 5 4 3 2 1

Authorised Representative: Easy Access System Europe - Mustamäe tee 50,
10621 Tallinn, Estonia, gpsr.requests@easproject.com

FSC www.fsc.org

MIX
Paper | Supporting
responsible forestry
FSC® C104723

THE POETRY WORLD OF JOHN AGARD

ILLUSTRATED BY SHIRLEY HOTTIER

Otter-Barry BOOKS

Contents

Introduction by Darren Chetty

John Agard's first book of poetry for children was called
I Din Do Nuttin. It was published in 1983, when I was still
at primary school. Most of the poetry I read then was about
flowers and nature. There are some very good poems about
flowers and nature. But John's poetry showed me that poems
could be about lots of other things too.

When I became a primary school teacher it was one of
the books I always shared with the children in my class.
Sometimes I read the poems aloud. Sometimes we all read
them together.

I Din Do Nuttin is a phrase in the Caribbean Creole of
Guyana, where John was born. Some of the children in my class
would recognise this phrase. It was often the first time they had
read or heard Caribbean Creole in their school in England.

My own parents are not from the Caribbean, but I can
relate to hearing different words and phrases in school and at
home – maybe you can too. Listen to the language in John's
poems: '*A thank-you can break no bone*', '*Bad dancer mustn't
blame the floor*' and my favourite '*Hurry hurry mek bad
curry*'. What are the phrases that you hear at home?

John shows us that those sayings our parents and
grandparents use, the ones that can sound a bit unusual to us,
are special. They're worth holding on to. They're little bits of
history, which we can take and weave into poems. And they
contain golden nuggets of wisdom too - '*no rain, no rainbow*'.

In *The Poet's Pen*, John tells us he is '*a hunter with a pen...*

tracking down words'. I think that's a very good thing to be. In *My Camera*, he tells us his camera is his eye. He shows us how important it is to notice things. You know all those everyday things that other people might take for granted? Well, for John these become the stuff of poems.

John also notices how some people can be left out of things. For instance, Dilroy's eighth birthday is a happy occasion. He's got a pair of skates he wanted for a long, long time. But he still has a question:

But, Mummy, tell me why
They don't put a little boy
That looks a bit like me.
Why the boy on the card so white?

In the poetry world of John Agard, there's enough space for us all to be noticed and included. There's space for the things we say and hear, the games we play, and our pets. There's space for the questions we have and all the ideas in our imagination.

In *Friends on a Shelf*, John tells us *Books are friends*. I hope that **The Poetry World of John Agard** becomes your friend, just like John's first book became a friend to me. And after you've spent some time treating it like a friend – listening, noticing and joining in – maybe you'll feel like writing something yourself, and creating your own poetry world.

Darren Chetty

From

I Din Do Nuttin

8

I DIN DO NUTTIN WAS MY FIRST collection of poems
for children.

When I came to Britain in 1977 with my poet wife,
Grace Nichols and our daughter, Lesley, I was already in my
twenties, so my childhood memories were very much rooted in
Guyana, South America, where I was born and educated.

As I started going to schools all round the UK, giving talks for
the Commonwealth Institute, I came across things that were
unfamiliar, yet took me back to my own childhood.

Take the 'lollipop lady', for example. I immediately thought
this must be a lady who sells lollipops outside the school, the
way the 'sugarcake lady', as we called her, would sit outside my
primary school gate with her tray of goodies, which included
sliced mangoes with a pinch of salt, and 'sugarcake', made from
grated coconut. Of course, I soon realised that the lollipop lady
got her name from the shape of her traffic-stopping stick, which
inspired the poem *Lollipop Lady*.

Coming from a country without winter, I was looking forward
to seeing snow and that inspired If *Only I Could Take Home A
Snowflake*. But you can be inspired in all sorts of ways. From
little scraps of everyday conversation (*I Din Do Nuttin*) to
imagining a little black boy reflecting on his birthday card, as in
Happy Birthday, Delroy.

John

9

I Din Do Nuttin

I din do nuttin
I din do nuttin
I din do nuttin.
All I did
was throw Granny pin
in the rubbish bin.

I din do nuttin
I din do nuttin
I din do nuttin.
All I did
was mix paint in
Mammy biscuit tin.

I din do nuttin
I din do nuttin.

New Shoes

Buying new shoes
takes so long.
When the colour is right
the size is wrong.

The lady asks,
'How does it fit?'
I say to Mum,
'Pinches a bit.'

But that's not true
It's just because
I don't want the brown
I prefer the blue.

The lady goes inside
brings another size
this time the blue.
Not too big. Not too tight.

As you guessed
Just right, just right.
Mum says, 'The blue will do.'
And I agree. Don't you?

Stop Troubling that Phone

Telephone,
telephone,
you're so alone

Like a king
with no throne

Like a dog
with no bone.

Telephone,
telephone,
you look so bored.

Nothing to do,
Nobody's even talking to you,
I guess I'd better play with you.

Ask Mummy ask Daddy

When I ask Daddy
Daddy says ask Mummy.

When I ask Mummy
Mummy says ask Daddy.
I don't know where to go.

Better ask my teddy
he never says no.

cat in

Look at that!
Look at that!

But when you look
there's no cat.

Without a purr
just a flash of fur
and gone
like a ghost.

he Dark

The most
you see
are two tiny
green traffic lights
staring at the night.

Lollipop Lady

Lollipop lady,
lollipop lady
wave your magic stick
and make the traffic
stop a while
so we can cross the street.

Trucks and cars
rushing past
have no time for little feet.
They hate to wait
especially when late
but we'll be late too
except for you.

So lollipop lady,
lollipop lady,
in the middle of the street
wave your magic stick
and make the traffic
give way to little feet.

Mother Alligator's Advice to her children

Don't eat too much sweet
You'll spoil your lovely teeth.

Don't touch jelly or treacle
Stick to eating people.

If I could Only Take Home a Snowflake

Snowflakes
like tiny
insects
drifting
down.

Without a hum
they come.
Without a hum
they go.

Snowflakes
like tiny
insects
drifting
down.

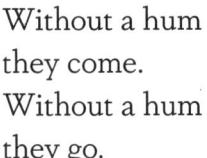

If only
I could take
one
home with me
to show
my friends
in the sun,
just for fun,
just for fun.

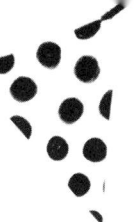

Happy Birthday, Dilroy

My name is Dilroy.
I'm a little black boy
and I'm eight today.

My birthday cards say
it's great to be eight
and they sure right
coz I got a pair of skates
I want for a long long time.

My birthday cards say,
Happy Birthday, Dilroy!
But, Mummy, tell me why
they don't put a little boy
that looks a bit like me.
Why the boy on the card so white?

From
Say It Again, Granny

SINCE THE CARIBBEAN IS A MIX OF PEOPLE from different continents, you'll find a variety of influences on the way people use language. In the English-speaking Caribbean, you'll hear English spoken in a formal situation. However, just take a walk to the market, or listen to calypso or reggae music, and often you will hear English words spoken with West African turns and rhythms.

In this Creole language, as it is called, you'll find English words you recognise, but the words are put together in an unusual way, forming poetic expressions. For 'greedy' you might hear 'wanty-wanty.' For tears you might hear 'eye-water.' For the 'sole' of your feet, you might hear 'foot-bottom'.

These examples are from the English-speaking Caribbean. But a Creole language is also spoken in the Dutch, French and Spanish

Caribbean. And since Creole is the spoken language of the people, it's no surprise that Creole holds a rich storehouse of proverbs.

Proverbs are old sayings, passed from generation to generation, mostly by word of mouth, and are said to be the salt of speech because they flavour your speech without wasting words. You could also say that poetry is the salt of language, adding new flavour to everyday words, and in a poem you don't want to waste words.

In *Say It Again, Granny*, the poems are in the voice of a girl or boy, who is growing up in Britain but whose grandmother is from the Caribbean. The grandmother is always expressing herself through proverbs. Some of the Caribbean Creole proverbs the grandmother uses may also remind you of proverbs you already know, for proverbs can be found in cultures across the world.

'More haste, less speed' is an English proverb you might have heard said as warning to people who are forever in a rush. Well, the grandmother in *Say It Again, Granny* puts it like this: *Hurry-Hurry Mek Bad Curry.*

John

The Older the Violin the Sweeter the Tune

Me Granny old
Me Granny wise
stories shine like a moon
from inside she eyes.

Me Granny can dance
Me Granny can sing
but she can't play violin.

Yet she always saying,
'Dih older dih violin
de sweeter de tune.'

Me Granny must be wiser
than the man inside the moon.

A Thank-you Can Break No Bone

When I forget my manners
in the street
or at home

Granny would remind me
'A howdee-do can't hurt you
and a thank-you can break no bone.
Who knows
a please might yet get you
that ice-cream cone.'

Thank you, Granny,
Thank you.

I want another one, please.

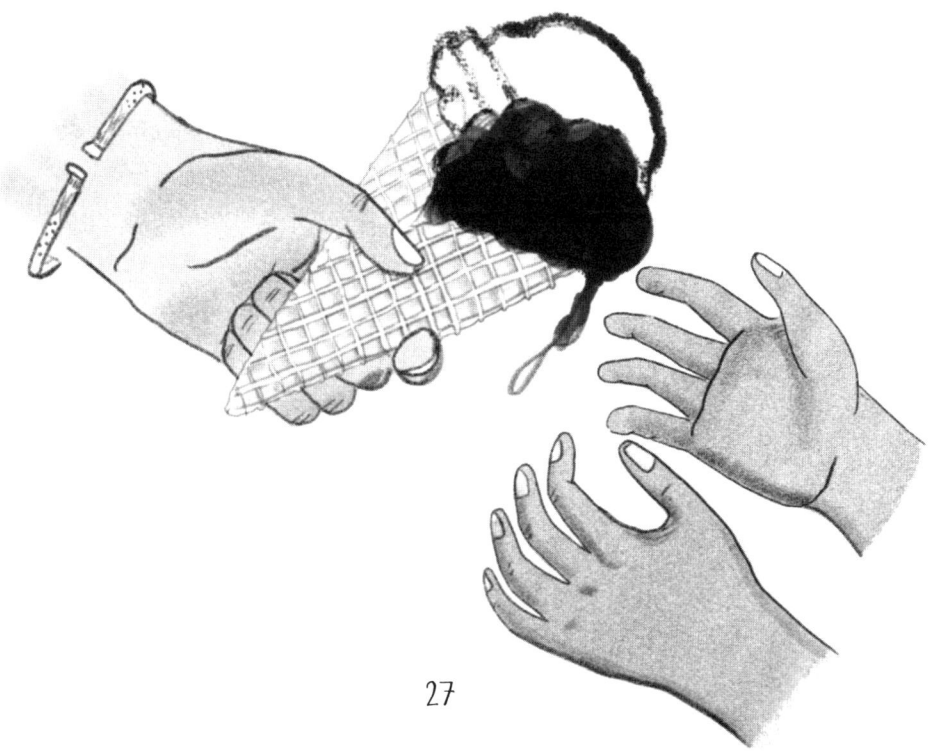

Mouth Open, Story Jump Out

Mouth open
story jump out

I tell you me secret
you let it out

But I don't care
if the world hear
shout it out

Mouth open
story jump out

Besides,
the secret I tell you
wasn't even true
so you can shout
till you blue

So boo
mouth open
story jump out.

Don't Count Your Chickens Before They Hatch

I know Granny always saying
when you look forward to something too much
you might be disappointed

But I'm really looking forward
to that new bike,
and when I get that new bike
watch me ride it in the day
watch me ride it in the night
watch me do a wheely in the wind
watch me fancy up a swerve
watch me race and spin.

Nobody going catch me
Nobody
Just watch...

Granny would just smile and say,
'Better don't count your chickens before they hatch.'

But Granny I'm sorry to say
I have a secret to tell

I count me chicks every day
I count them one to ten

so cosy in their egg-house
under warm mother hen.

Hurry-Hurry Mek Bad Curry

People rushing
people pushing
people in a big haste
people in a big speed
not taking their time
like a little seed.

Why all the hurry?
Why all the flurry?
Why all the scurry?

Me Granny does always say,
'Hurry-hurry mek bad curry.'

One Finger Can't Catch Flea

One finger can wiggle
One finger can tickle
But have you ever seen
a one-finger snap?

One hand can wave
One hand can flap
But have you ever seen
a one-hand clap?

One finger can pat a cat
One finger can stroke a dog
But I'm sure you'll agree with my Granny
that one finger can't ketch flea.

So let's work together, you and me,
like two hands from one body.

Who the cap Fit, Let Them wear it

If it wasn't you
who tek de chalk
and mark up de wall
juggle with de egg
and mek it fall
then why you didn't answer
when you hear Granny call?

If it wasn't you
who bounce yuh ball
in de goldfish bowl
wipe mud from yuh shoes
all over de floor
and poke yuh finger
straight in de butter

If it wasn't you
then why yuh heart a-flutter?
Why yuh voice a-stutter?
And why you look so jumpy
when you stand up in front of Granny?

'Who the cap fit,
let dem wear it.'
That's what Granny does always say
and that she wasn't born yesterday.

No Rain, No Rainbow

Suppose today
you're feeling down
your face propping a frown.

Suppose today
you're one streak of a shadow
the sky giving you a headache.

Tomorrow
you never know
you might wake up
in the peak of a glow.

If you don't get the rain
how can you get the rainbow?

Say it again, Granny,
No rain, no rainbow.

Say it again, Granny,
No rain, no rainbow.

Bad Dancer
Mustn't Blame the Floor

You don't have to go to school
to know that bad workers
quarrel with their tools.

So if you make a kite
that's just too heavy
will you blame the wind
for being too light?

So if you make a boat
that just wouldn't float
will you say again
the wind wasn't right?

And if you make a chair
with legs so rickety and thin
when you sit you tumble right in
will you take it with a grin
or will you swear
at the chair
and blame the hammer and nail?

Well, me Granny would just tell you,
'Bad dancer mustn't blame the floor.'

So when music sweet
just move your feet

and don't bother blame the floor.

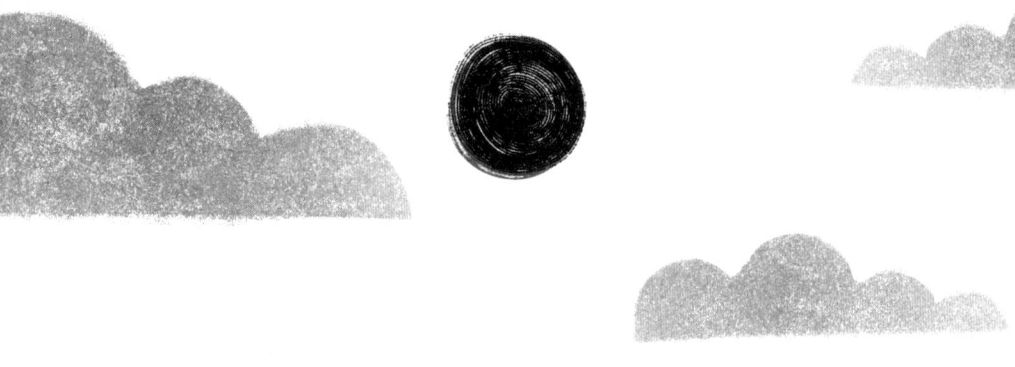

From

No Hickory No Dickory No Dock

LONG BEFORE POEMS were written down, poems were sung, even danced to. Not surprisingly, nursery rhymes with their robust rhythms were first recited and sung before they were written down.

Think of 'Rock-a-bye Baby on the Tree Top', sung as a lullaby, or 'Ring-a-ring-a-roses' chanted as a ring game.

In the Caribbean, there are also rhymes chanted as part of ring-play on moonlight nights, or skipping rope rhymes chanted in the schoolyard.

Like me, my wife, the poet Grace Nichols, also grew up in Guyana where we learnt English nursery rhymes. So we thought we'd both have some fun making up nursery rhymes with a Caribbean flavour.

Together we did *No Hickory No Dickory No Dock*, a collection of Caribbean nursery rhymes that also play with well-known English ones. Along with our own poems, we included rhymes passed down in the oral tradition.

Here's an example:

Mosquito one
Mosquito Two
Mosquito jump
In de old man shoe.

So-So Joe

So-So Joe
de so-so man
wore a so-so suit
with a so-so shoe.
So-So Joe
de so-so man
lived in a so-so house
with a so-so view.
And when you asked
So-so Joe
de so-so man:
'How do you do?'
So-So Joe
de so-so man
would say to you:
'Just so-so
Nothing new.'

Give me Five

Give me five fingers of joy
Give me five fingers of joy
Give me five fingers of joy
from every jumping girl and boy

Give me five fingers of love
Give me five fingers of love
Give me five fingers of love
from the side below and above

Give me five fingers of play
Give me five fingers of play
Give me five fingers of play
I tell you that will make my day

Fingers tell a story
Fingers tell their very own story
O yes believe me
O yes believe me
Fingers tell a story
Fingers tell their very own story

Catch the morning with open hands
Catch the morning with open hands
Catch the morning with open hands
Today we leave our fists behind

Skipping Rope Spell

Turn rope turn

Don't trip my feet

Turn rope turn

for my skipping feet

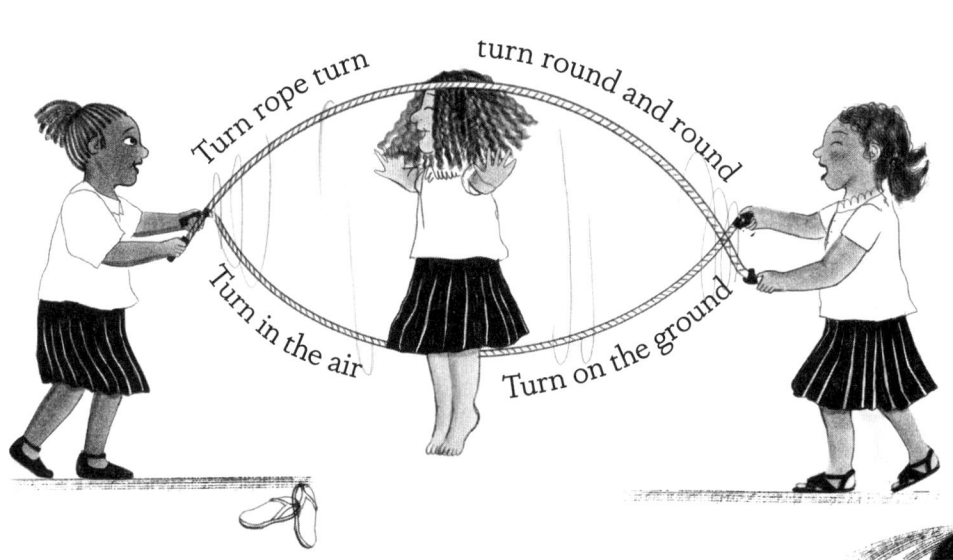

Turn rope turn   turn round and round

Turn in the air   Turn on the ground

One for your high

One for your low

Turn rope turn

Not too fast, not too slow

Turn rope turn

turn to the north

turn to the south

But please rope, please,

Don't make me OUT!

No Hickory No Dickory No Dock

Wasn't me
Wasn't me
said the little mouse
I didn't run up no clock

You could hickory me
You could dickory me
or lock me in a dock

I still say
I didn't run up no clock

Was me who ran under your bed
Was me who bit into your bread
Was me who nibbled your cheese

But please please,
I didn't run up no clock
no hickory
no dickory
no dock.

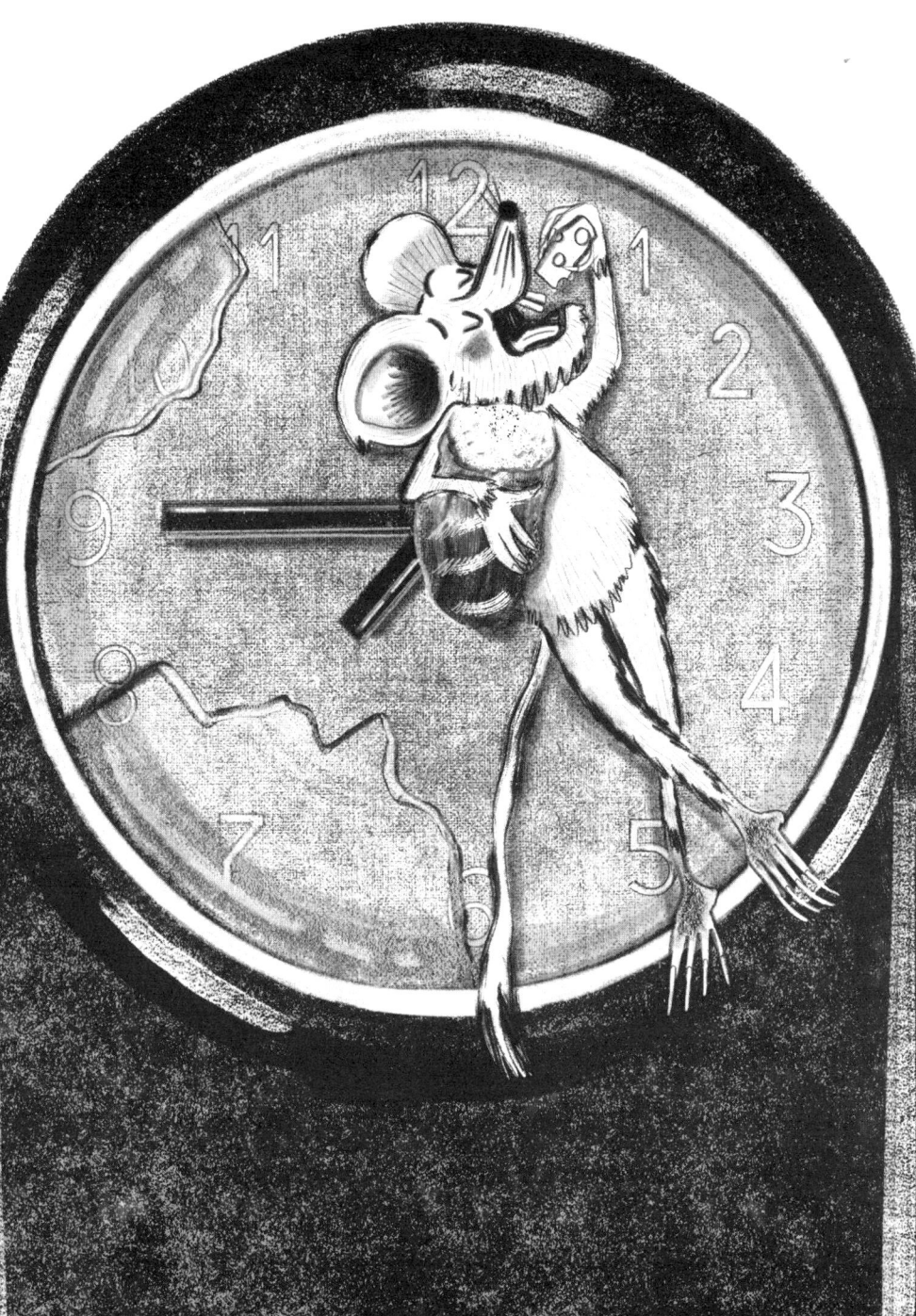

What Turkey Doing?

Mosquito one
mosquito two
mosquito jump
in de old man shoe

Cockroach three
cockroach four
cockroach dance thru
a crack in de floor

Spider five
spider six
spider weaving
a web of tricks

Monkey seven
monkey eight
monkey playing with
pencil and slate

Turkey nine
turkey ten
what turkey doing
in chicken pen?

Ladybird Ladybird

Ladybird
Ladybird

Have you heard
the birds
laughing?
They say you can't sing

But ladybird
I don't care
if you can't sing,
I like how you move
your red and black wing.

woodpecker

Carving
tap/tap
music
out of
tap/tap
tree trunk
keep me
busy
whole day
tap/tap
long

tap/tap
pecker
birdsong
tap/tap
pecker
birdsong

48

tree bark
is tap/tap
drumskin
fo me beak
I keep
tap/tap
rhythm
fo forest
heartbeat

tap/tap
chisel beak
long
tap/tap
honey leak
song
pecker/tap
tapper/peck
pecker
birdsong.

Cow Chat

Mama Moo
Papa Moo
Baby Moo
lying in the grass

Said Mama Moo
to Papa Moo
'When the grass is new
I love to chew'

'And I do too'
said Baby Moo.

Twinkle Twinkle Firefly

Twinkle
Twinkle
Firefly
In the dark
It's you I spy

Over the river
Over the bush

Twinkle
Twinkle
Firefly
For the traveller
passing by

Over the river
Over the bush

Twinkle
Twinkle
Firefly
Lend the dark
your sparkling eye.

From

Laughter is an Egg

SOMETIMES THERE MIGHT BE A TITLE for a collection in your head, though you haven't even written the poems. You don't know down which road the title will lead you, yet the title keeps haunting you and propelling you towards poems. This happened with *Laughter is an Egg*.

It just goes to show how words breed words, how words pollinate into words. In the world of the imagination, there are no one-way streets. You travel wherever your imagination compels you.

One thought going through my mind was that people speak of cracking eggs and cracking jokes, and without laughter in our lives we ourselves would crack up.

In mythology, you also hear of the great cosmic egg, cracking into two halves, the top half giving birth to the heavens, the bottom half giving birth to the earth. This got me thinking of Laughter as a creative trickster in the guise of an egg, for an egg is life, and laughter likewise is life.

In a poem, an ordinary happening can be transformed, if hopefully, you manage to get the right words in the right order. Once I visited a school that was celebrating 'Book Week' and the teachers came all dressed up as their favourite Book characters. When the headmaster appeared as Fungus The Bogeyman, I thought to myself there's a poem in that. Out of that experience came *Bogeyman Headmaster*.

Once Upon a Time

Once upon a time there lived
a small joke
in the middle of nowhere.

This small joke
was dying to share
itself with someone

but nobody came to hear
this small joke.

So this small joke
told itself to the birds

and the birds told this small joke to the trees
and the trees told this small joke to the rivers
and the rivers told this small joke to the mountains
and the mountains told this small joke to the stars

till the whole world
started to swell with laughter

and nobody believed
it all began
with a small joke

that lived in the middle of nowhere.

Everybody kept saying

it was me
it was me.

Laughter is an Egg

Laughter is an egg
that does a one-leg hop

Laughter is an egg
that can outspin a top

Laughter is an egg
with a crick-crack face

that can hide in the heart
of the human race.

Where Does Laughter Begin?

Does it start in your head
and spread to your toe?

Does it start in your cheeks
and grow downwards so
till your knees feel weak?

Does it start with a tickle
in your tummy so
till you want to jump right out

of all your skin?
Or does laughter simply begin

with your mouth?

Hatch Me a Riddle

In a little white room
all round and smooth
sits a yellow moon.

In a little white room
once open, for ever open,
sits a yellow moon.

In a little white room,
with neither window nor door,
sits a yellow moon.

Who will break the walls
of the little white room
to steal the yellow moon?

A wise one or a fool?

Prayer to Laughter

O Laughter
giver of relaxed mouths

you who rule our belly with tickles
you who come when not called
you who can embarrass us at times

send us stitches in our sides
shake us till the water reaches our eyes
buckle our knees till we cannot stand

we whose faces are grim and shattered
we whose hearts are no longer hearty
O Laughter we beg you

crack us up
crack us up.

Bogeyman Headmaster

Our headmaster is a bogeyman
Our headmaster is a bogeyman
and he'll catch you if he can.

He creeps through the window
when the school is closed at night
just to give the caretaker a fright.

Our headmaster is a bogeyman
Our headmaster is a bogeyman
and he'll catch you if he can.

When he walks
his feet never touch the ground.
When he talks
his mouth never makes a sound.
That's why assembly is so much fun.

You should see him float through the air
when we say our morning prayer
and at assembly the teachers get trembly
when the piano starts to play on its own.
It's our bogeyman headmaster having a bogeyman joke.

Laughter Will Return

The old man and old woman cried
when their dog died.
They had that dog from a pup.
They watched that dog grow up.

That dog was once their friend.
Now that dog is dead.

From the house of the dead
Laughter has gone.
To the house of the dead
Laughter will return.

Laughter and the Elements

Fire and Water
Wind and Earth

These four elements
I will forge into myself
said Laughter

Till the wind of breath
will fill your lungs.

Till the water of tears
will flood your eyes

Till the fire of blood
will flush your face

Till the whole of your body
will roll on earth

your legs weak with giggles.

Egg-and-Spoon Race

One school sports day,
in the egg-and-spoon race,
the egg ran away
from the spoon.

The egg brought first place
but the judges said: 'Let's disqualify
the egg.
It should have waited on the spoon.'

The egg said: 'Why not disqualify
the spoon
for not catching up with me?
I'll never understand the mystery
of the human race.'

From
Grandfather's Old Bruk-a-Down Car

LOOK AROUND. And you'll see objects everywhere. The chair you sit on. The cup you drink from, the pen you write with. Some objects, like those just mentioned, are there for practical uses. Say a Pebble collected from a beach, might have no visible usefulness. But it can still fill your inside with a sense of calmness and bring back memories, even the smells, of a happy day beside the sea.

While it is true that people can become possessed by the objects they possess, objects hold stories and memories. The poems in *Grandfather's Old Bruk-a-Down Car* tell of different

objects that are special to different people. For example, one poem was inspired by a typewriter and my mother herself was a typist, skilled at shorthand. I remember her over her typewriter with carbon paper. Have you a favourite object that means a lot to you? Well, that object might also inspire you to write a poem.

I dedicated this collection to my English teacher, Father Stanley Maxwell; a Scottish priest who taught us for our O-level exams at my secondary school, St Stanislavs, in Georgetown, Guyana. Among the boys, he was known as Maxy. Part of the dedication reads: 'To Maxy who made the dictionary an adventure.'

English was my favourite subject. Father Maxwell had the habit of going through the dictionary and writing words on the blackboard for us to remember. He would give us funny clues to words that were strange to us. He made the dictionary into a game. We would try to test him with weird words, but he seemed to know every word in the dictionary. We could never catch him out. Once, I said, "Sir, what's whippersnapper?" Maxy looked at me and said, "Agard, look in the mirror." What better way to learn the meaning of whippersnapper than by looking in the mirror, aged 13.

Don't just get hooked on your computer spell check. Look through the pages of the dictionary for yourself and adventure awaits. *John*

Grandfather's Old Bruk-a-Down Car

It does make a lot of smoke
and people like to joke
about my grandfather's old bruk-a-down car.

It can only run slow
but it still can go
my grandfather's old bruk-a-down car.

It mightn't go fast
but it can still travel far
my grandfather's old bruk-a-down car.

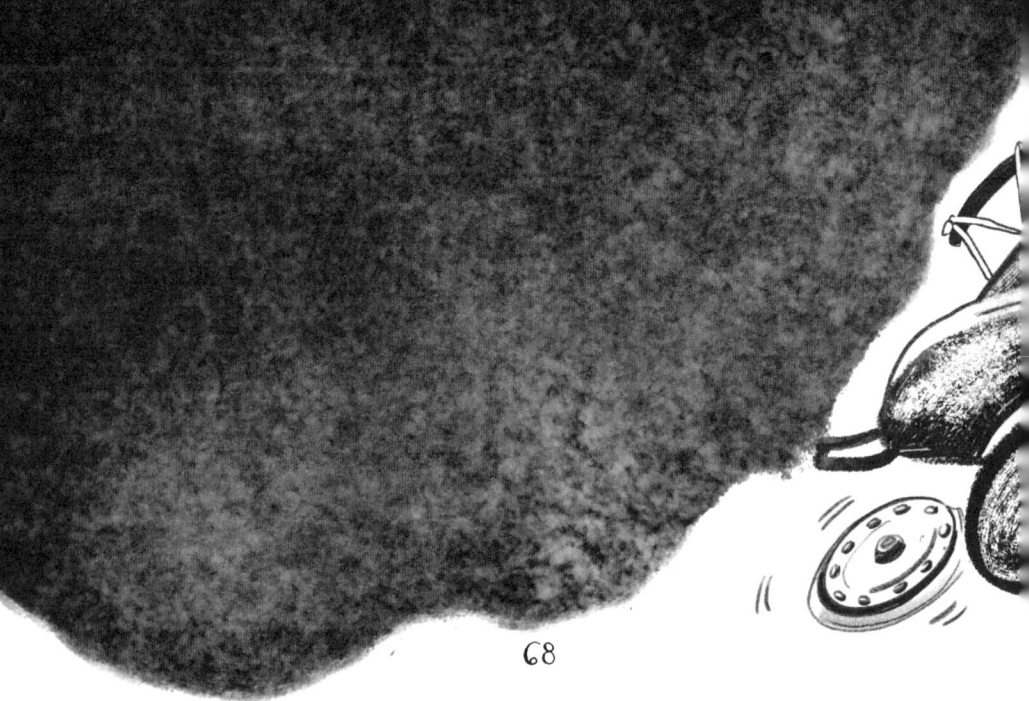

It does make a racket
every time he try to start it
my grandfather's old bruk-a-down car.

He does have to crank it and crank it
and when at last the engine rev-up
he does thank it and thank it.

People would tease him by calling
his old bruk-a-down car 'SCRAP-IRON'
but my grandfather calls it 'MY STALLION'.

My Wellies

They've splashed
up puddles

They've mashed
up mud

They've skipped
on leaves

They've tripped
on roots

They've hopped
with grasshoppers

And I wouldn't swop
them for anything

Not these smelly old wellies
that once belonged to a garden gnome.

Mum's Typewriter

Mum is a wizard
on a typewriter.
An absolute ace.
There's one she keeps
in an old grey case.
Letters come out by leaps
on to the page
until rows of words
go marching by neat-neat.

Mum is a tapdancer
on typewriter keys
but she uses fingers
instead of her feet.
Sometimes she lets me
have a go.
But I'm not so quick.
One thing I know though,
she won't swop
her old manual
for a new electric.

My Mum gives her typewriter
a little hug
and says: 'This old faithful
will never need a plug.'

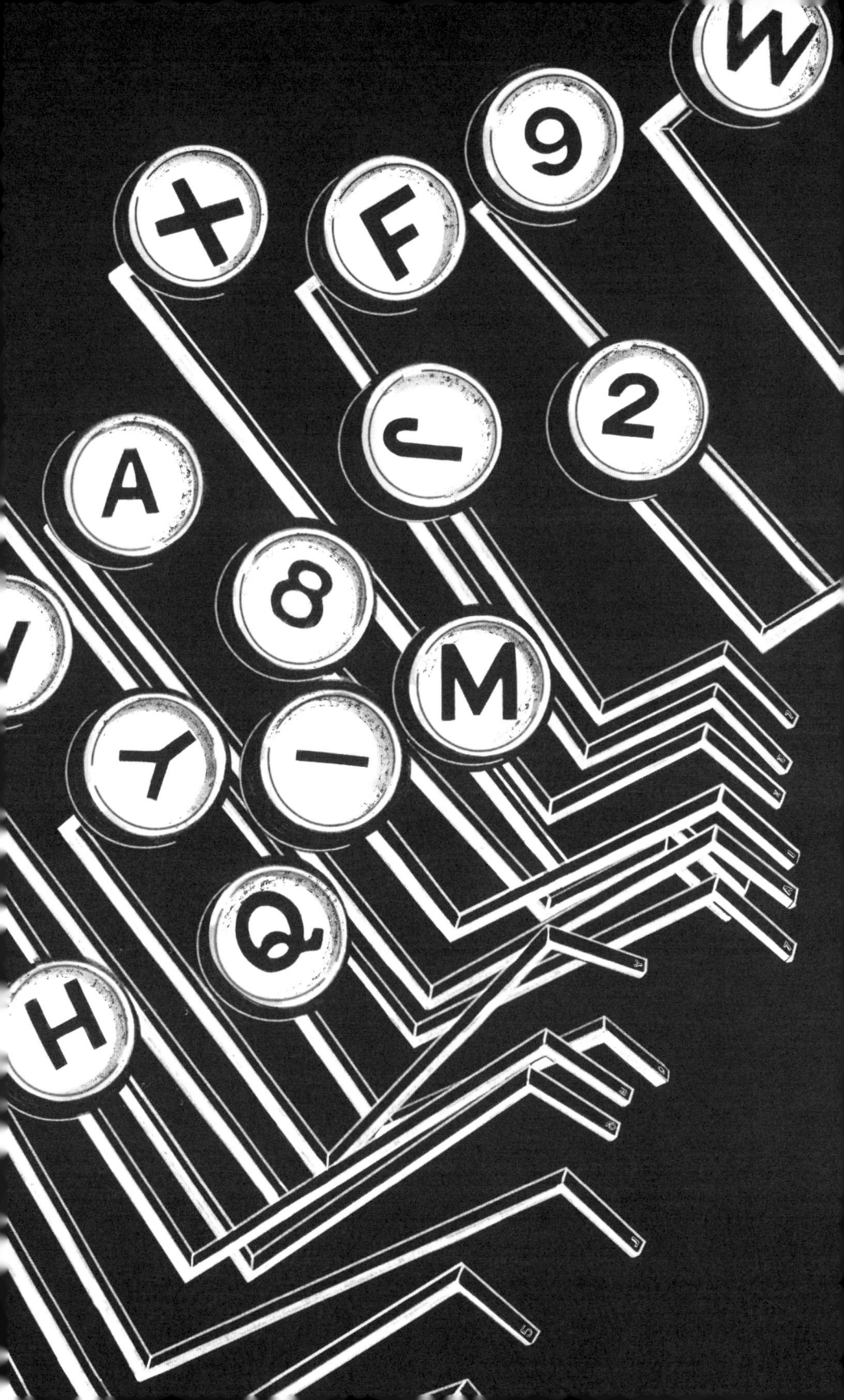

Gramma's Biscuit Tin

Gramma's biscuit tin
beside her bed
has odds and ends
like covers
that once belonged to pens
and letters
from old-old friends.

Gramma's biscuit tin
beside her bed
has bits and pieces
like keys
that once belonged to locks
and screws
from broken clocks.

Gramma's biscuit tin
beside her bed
has all sorts of things
like rings
that once belonged to curtains
and fuses
from forgotten plugs.

And Gramma uses
that biscuit tin
beside her bed
for keeping her bingo card.
She prays to the Lord
that one day she'll win.
But win or lose
her dreams are in
that biscuit tin.

74

My Camera

My camera
catches movement
slow or quick

My camera
has a shutter
but doesn't click

My camera
points to the ground
and takes out the sky

My camera
needs no film
but is a spy

My camera
(have you guessed?)
is my eye.

The Poet's Pen

I'm a hunter with a pen
and I'm tracking down words.

Some stay high as birds
Some keep low as worms.

But I'm armed with my pen
and I'll track words to their den.

Some words are snakes
I hear their hiss.

Some words are tigers
I hear their roar.

Some words are scorpions
Watch out for their sting.

But I'm hiding with my pen
and I'll catch them in a wink.

My God, I've run out of ink!

Auntie Nell's Grip

Auntie Nell got a suitcase. She calls it her grip.
Auntie Nell is forever going on some trip.

She been overland. She been oversea.
That suitcase seen more places than you or me.

She's always knocking on some relative's door.
Once, without warning, she showed up in Singapore.

The day she left her born-island Tobago
She said: 'Wherever I go, this grip got to go'.

Whenever she's not travelling all over the globe
Auntie Nell keeps her suitcase on top her wardrobe.

With a leather belt she'll strap it extra tight.
Then soon she and her grip are off on a flight.

The truth is Auntie Nell is scared of flying.
But she feels that lucky grip will keep her from dying.

Uncle Nedd's Alarm Clock

He doesn't keep it near his bed
to invade his dreaming head.

It doesn't make a ringing sound
to disturb his slumberdown.

It hasn't got a night-time glow
within sight of his pillow.

Oh no, says Uncle Nedd, twinkling his eyes.
I have a secret clock which helps me to rise.

It's a little cuckoo that never fails
and it sits among the branches of my brain.

I simply tell myself what time I'd like to wake
and my internal cuckoo gives me a shake.

The Speller's Bag

Here a bone.
Here a stone.
In my bag
I keep them all.

A stone brought me
by the sea.
A bone taken from where
I'll never tell thee.

A bone, a stone,
a feather, a shell,
all in my bag
to cast a spell.

A shell that taught
the wind to howl.
A feather stolen
from the back of an owl.

Then again it might be
from a raven's neck.
I'll never tell thee.

Look inside all who dare.

Inside my bag
you'll find your fear.

From

We Animals Would Like a Word With You

ANIMALS HAVE CONTRIBUTED to language. So have birds, fishes, insects. Oh yes, we have to thank our furred, feathered and scaly friends for many of the images and expressions used in everyday speech.

We call a spy a 'mole'. A constant reader is a 'bookworm'. We call a person who likes staying up late, a 'night owl'. Something suspicious is something 'fishy'.

Since the coming of electronic mail, letters through the post are now known as 'snail mail', while the competitive struggle for material power is known as the 'rat race'.

I couldn't help wondering what the rats had to say about all that. You could say a poem was starting to nibble. And after writing 'Rat Race' in the voice of the rats, I was inspired to write poems in the voices of other animals.

Try putting yourself in the voice of a four-footed friend. Or put yourself in the voice of a bird, a fish, an insect. Here's a chance for you to make words roar, chirp, buzz.

Rat Race

Rat race?
Don't make us laugh.
It's you humans
who're always in a haste.

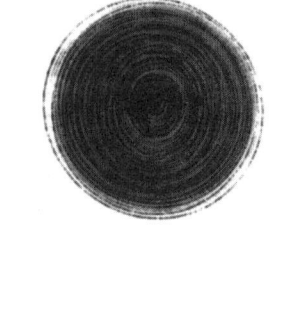

Ever seen a rat
in a bowler hat
rushing to catch a train?

Ever seen a rat
with a briefcase
hurrying through the rain?

And isn't it a fact
that all that hurry-hurry
gives you humans heart attacks?

No, my friend,
we rats relax.

Pass the cheese, please.

Bedbugs Marching Song

Bedbugs
Have the right
To bite.

Bedbugs
Of the world
Unite.

Don't let
These humans
Sleep too tight.

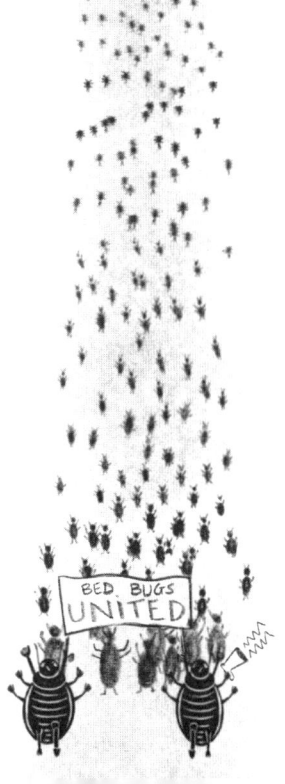

BED BUGS
UNITED

Goldfish Reflections

From this position
in my bowl
of glass
I watch time pass
like food crumbs falling
slow.

Faces come.
Faces go.
Some stare at me.
I watch the children grow.
I'm part of the family.
Once they moved my bowl
closer to the telly.
Reminded me of the sea
except for all the noise
and the running.

When they moved me back
to my spot by the curtain
I didn't feel so sad then.
Kept thinking
we're all in one big bowl.
They live in a bowl too.

Bats' Advice

Looking at life
from upside down
with your feet
to the sky
and your face
to the ground
you may ponder
the question
of how and why
and where you're from.
Make night your day
and day your night.
Bless the world
from upside down.

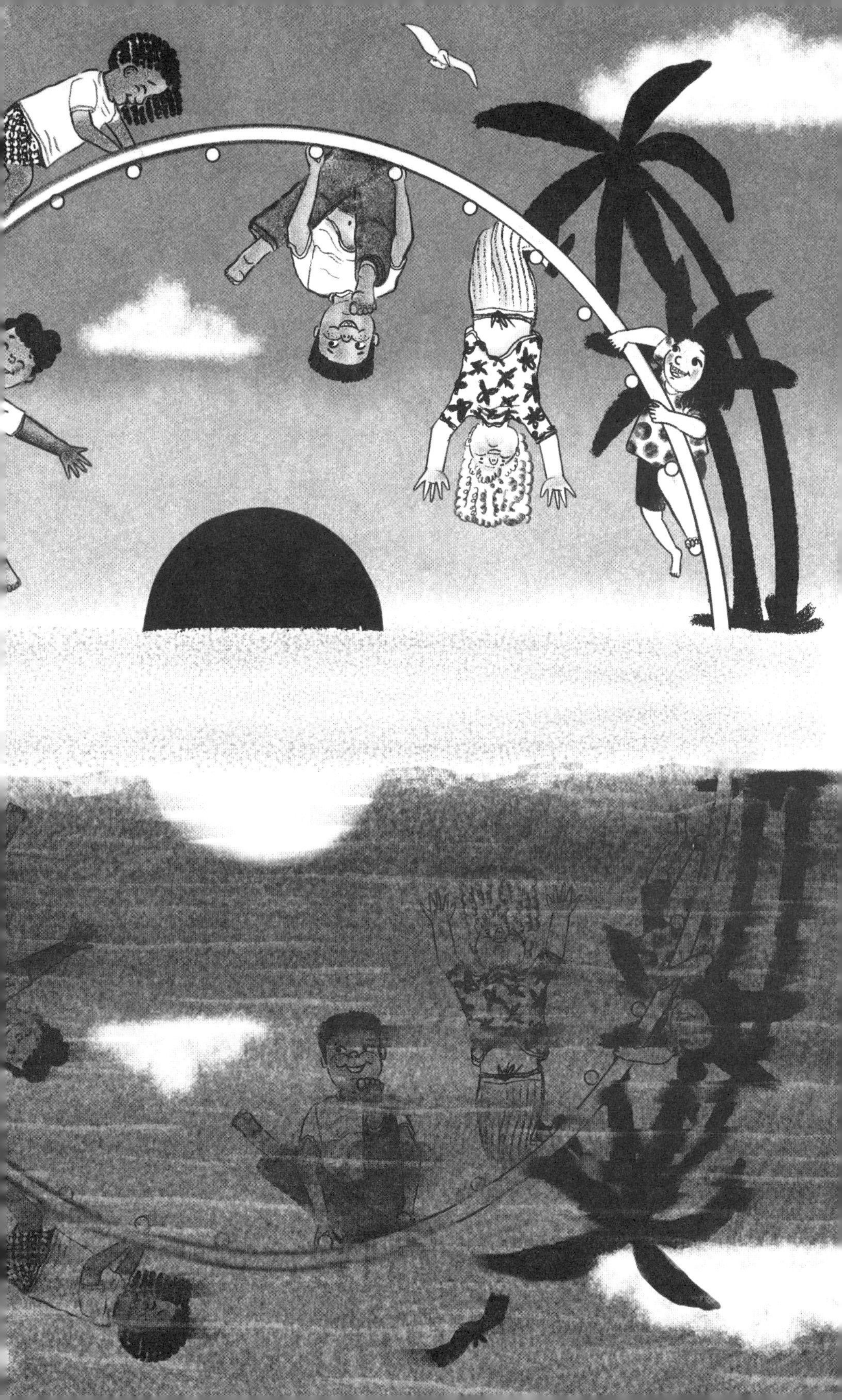

Insects Masquerade

Bet you didn't know
a broken twig could grow
two sudden wings and take off to the sky?
Unless you're a clever moth
camouflaged like a spy.

Bet you'd never guess
a thread
dangling
high
could begin
to
squirm.
That's me, Inchworm.

So you thought
I was a stick?
Until you tried to pick
me up. Then too quick
for your hands was I.
What a surprise
when you realised
I was no dry leaf
But a butterfly
making a fool of your eyes.

When will you humans learn
that we insects love disguise.

Hippo Writes a Love Poem to His Wife

Oh my beautiful fat wife
Larger to me than life
Smile broader than the river Nile
My winsome waddlesome
You do me proud in the shallow of morning
You do me proud in the deep of night
Oh, my bodysome mud-basking companion.

Hippo Writes a Love Poem to Her Husband

Oh my lubby-dubby hubby-hippo
With your widely winning lippo
My Sumo-thrasher of water
Dearer to me than any two-legger
How can I live without
Your ponderful potamous pout?

The Last Bird

I am becoming
the last bird
on the last branch
of the last tree
about to disappear
from the face of the earth.

The trees my friends, all gone.
Only empty holes
where trees used to be.
No more leaves to share
my secrets. All gone.
I am becoming
the last bird...

Suddenly, I wake
to a shake of wind.
I feel Mama's wing
her comforting beak
her feather-cosy breast.
Ah lucky me,
I'm safe in my nest.
Was only having a little bird's nightmare.

Yet why do I turn
again and again
as if waiting to hear
the deathly fall
of
a green-stealing rain?

Oh Mama
wing me
with your love.

Camel's Invitation

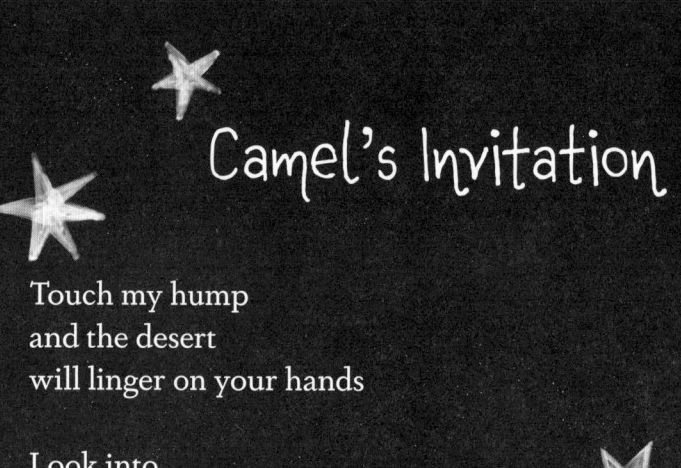

Touch my hump
and the desert
will linger on your hands

Look into
the good book of my eyes
And you will see a star
in the east
where the wise ones sit

Cradle the beast
that kneels on sand
and you will feel
such a beautiful thirst

From this day on
you will walk with your lips
to the sky.

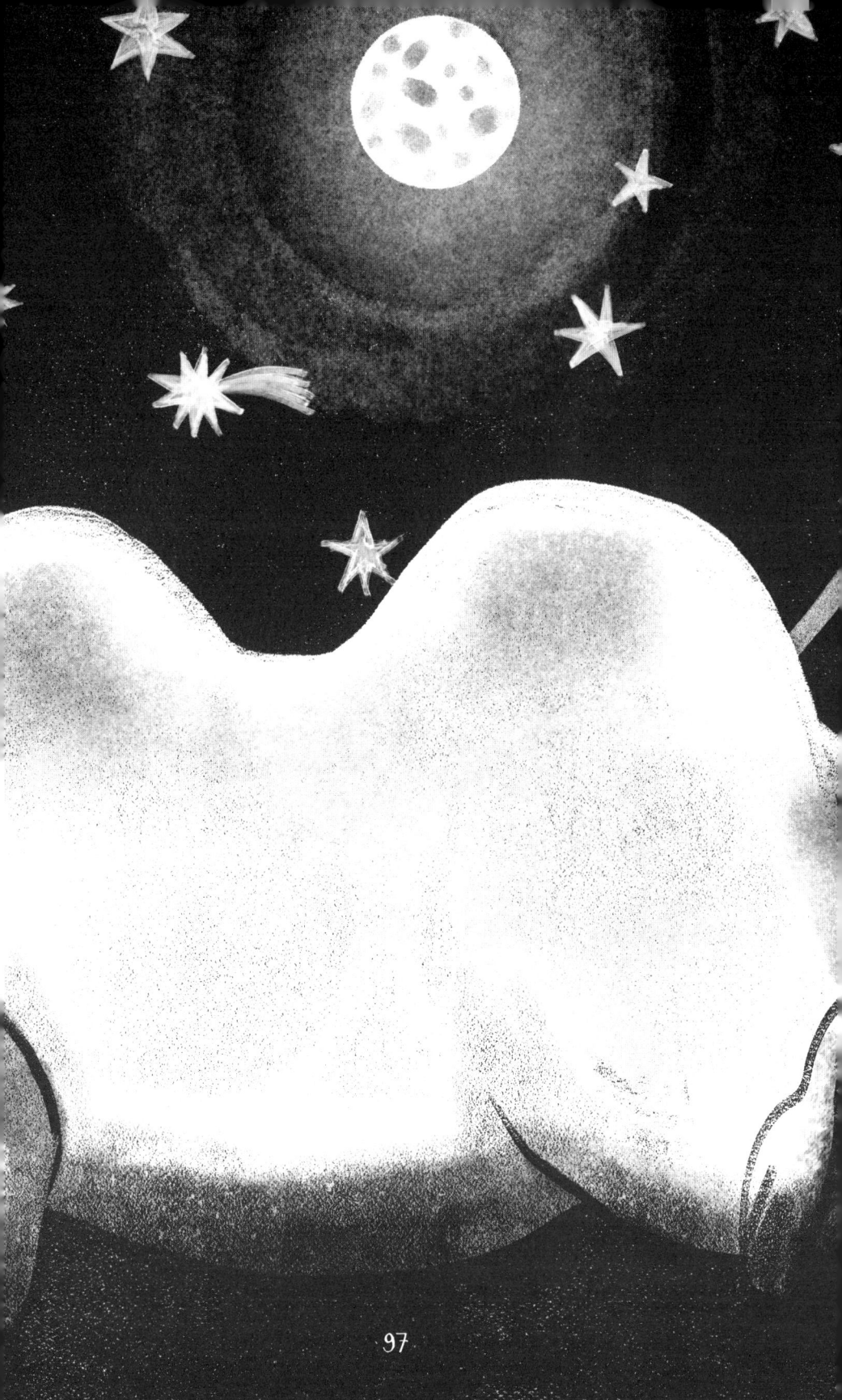

From
Come Back to me, my Boomerang

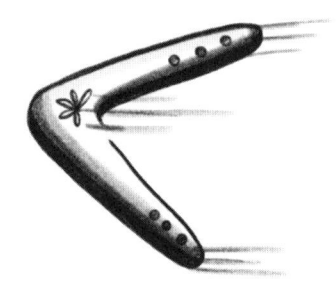

I OFTEN WRITE SEQUENCES OF POEMS about something that inspires me. A cluster, or a cycle, of poems that will, I hope, let the reader's imagination and mine meet and that we'll share in the journey of seeing something from different angles.

Speaking of angles, shapes are all around us: squares, circles, rectangles, triangles.

While walking across a pedestrian crossing, we're walking across horizontal rectangles. When we eat a doughnut we're scoffing a circle!

In our Mother's womb we experience our first moon-circle.

Shapes help to shape us, without our even being aware that we're being shaped.

John

Come Back to me, my Boomerang

Come back to me, my boomerang
Come back to me as fast as you can.

I threw you from Down Under
All the way to Over Yonder
somewhere past Beyond.

I can't believe you're gone
And the wind will not answer
And the horizon isn't much help.

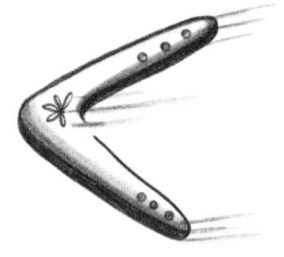

Come back to me, my boomerang
Come back to me as fast as you can.

I have no time to wait forever
and no more wood to make another.

Cone I Spy

I know a cone
that sits on the road
watching wheels
go by
and it's a traffic
cone I spy.

I know a cone
that brings to my lips
a strawberry
smile
and it's an ice-cream
cone I spy.

I know a cone
that falls with a seed
from a tree
standing high
and it's a pine
cone I spy.

One sits on the road among traffic and smoke.
One has no choice but to melt down my throat.
One could be a jewel on a Christmas tree,
but I keep it in the pocket of my coat
where the eyes of the world can never see.

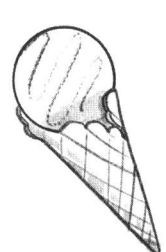
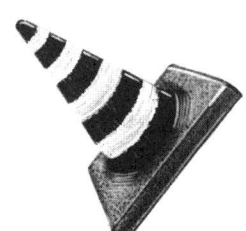

The Circle and the Square

Said the circle
to the square:
'It appears
your corners
are all the same.
I've counted four
and bet you can't roll
as I can do
when I'm a ball.'

Said the square
to the circle:
'Good luck to you,
but isn't it the truth
that a ball must bear
the kicks of a boot?
So you roll where you go,
I'll stay right here
and be a window.'

Said the circle
to the square:
'O what a pity
you can't come with me
when I rise to the air
as a nice bright bubble.
And wait till you see
the full-moon I can be,
the best of round and yellow.'

Said the square
to the circle:
'Bubbles burst, as you know,
and many a night,
the moon doesn't show.
I'm happy, thank you,
to be a window.
I enjoy the view.
I am my own little sky.
I am the house's eye.'

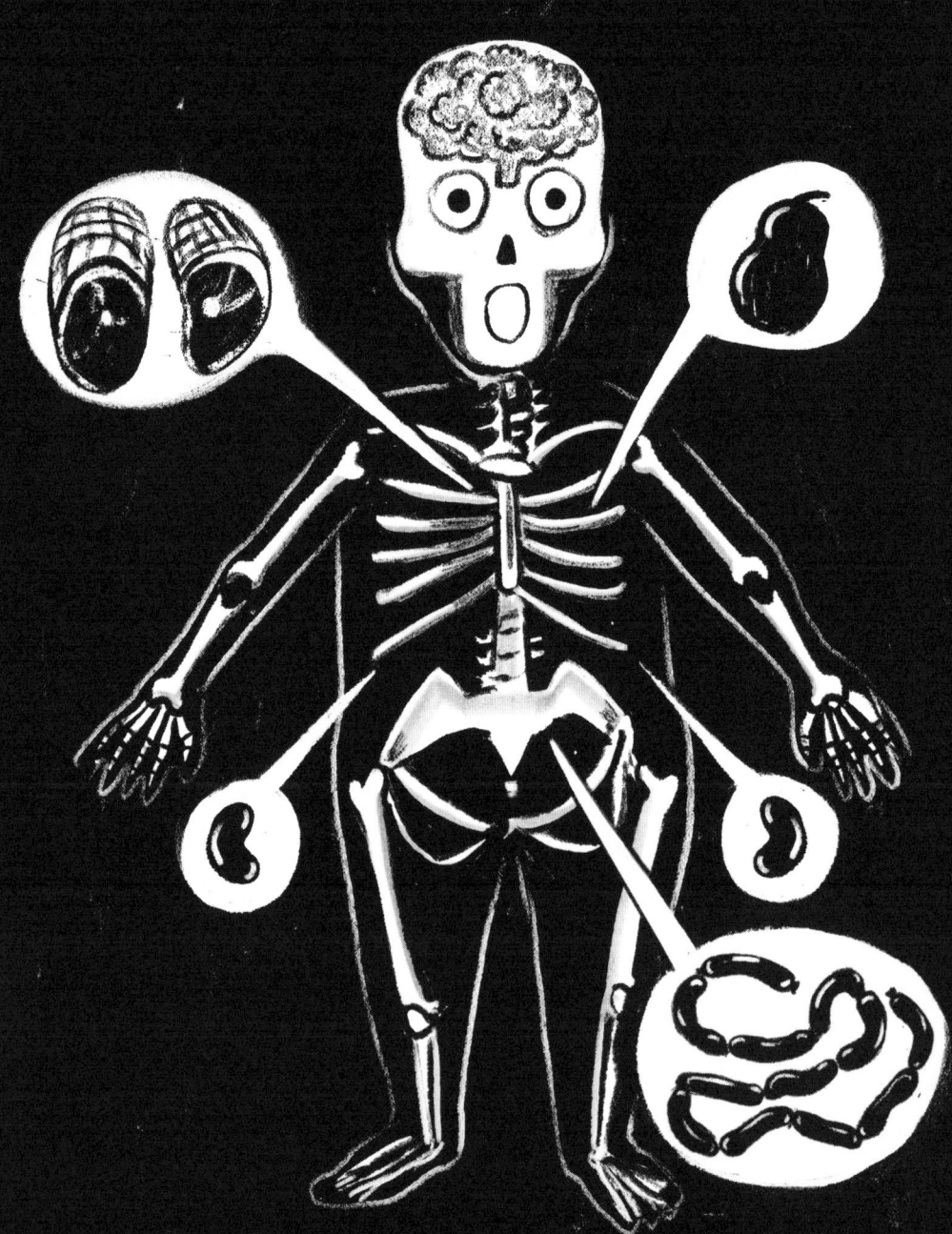

Inside of Me

I can't believe that jelly
cauliflower is my brain.

I can't believe that wriggly
sausage is my intestine.

I can't believe those gooey
red beans are my kidneys.

But they are mine, all mine.
Body parts that belong to me.

Yes, that throbbly pear
is actually my heart.

And my lungs, just there.
Why do they make me think of ham?

Please, no more diagrams
I'd rather not see

more of what's inside me.

Under the Arch

Under the arch
of a bridge -
Who tells the river flow on?

Under the arch
of its back -
Why does the cat purr a song?

Under the arch
of a rainbow -
How do you find a pot of gold?

Under the arch
of night flowers -
What makes a little gnome so bold?

Under the arch
of an eyebrow -
Why do eyes twinkle with questions?

Friends on a Shelf

Books are friends
that come
in squares
in rectangles
in oblongs.

They have no eyes
yet stare
from across a shelf.
They ask no questions
yet contain
a world of whys.
They have no ears
yet listen
when things go wrong.

Books are friends
that come
in squares
in rectangles
in oblongs

And even when I break
my promise to read them,
they will be there, waiting,
the moment I need them.

Mummy's Bump

Under her heart's thump-thump
sits Mummy's bump
a great huggy bump

and curled all cosy inside
could be my baby sister
could be my baby brother

having a water-ride
in the water-world
of Mummy's bump

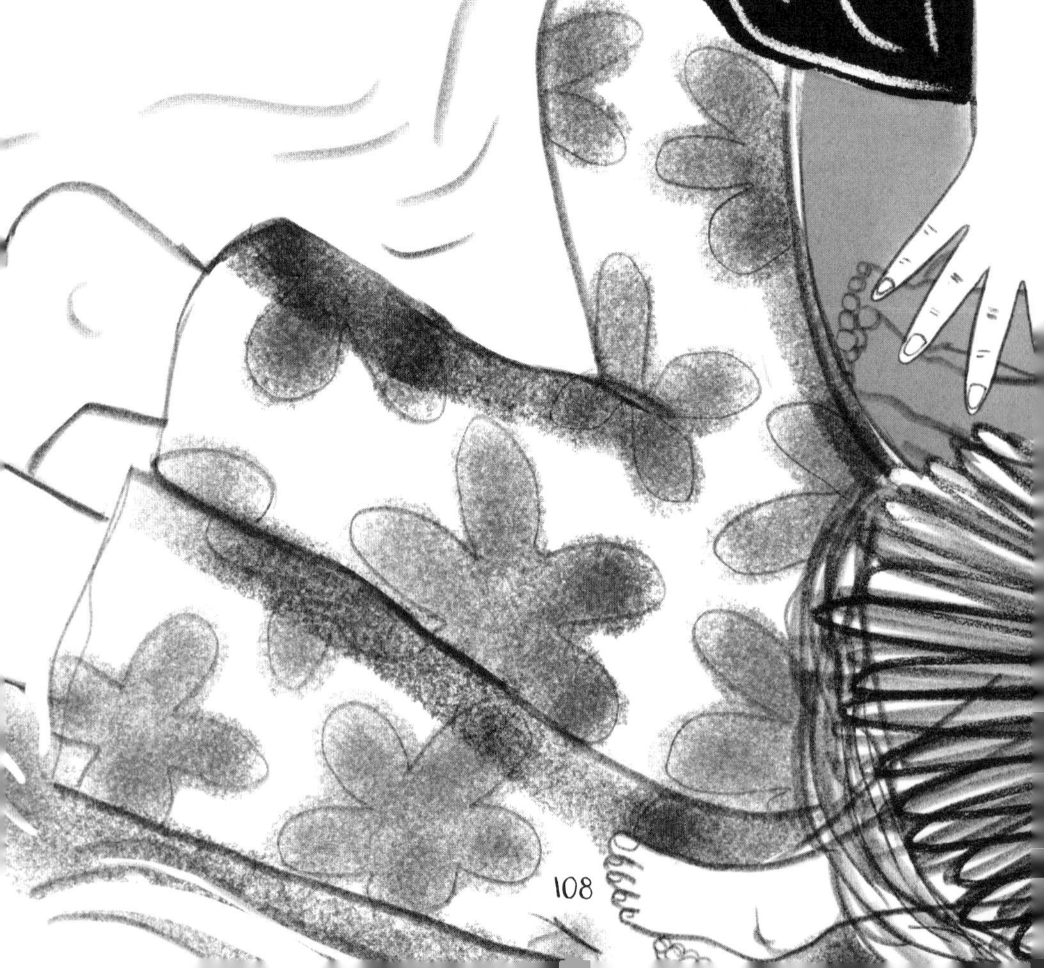

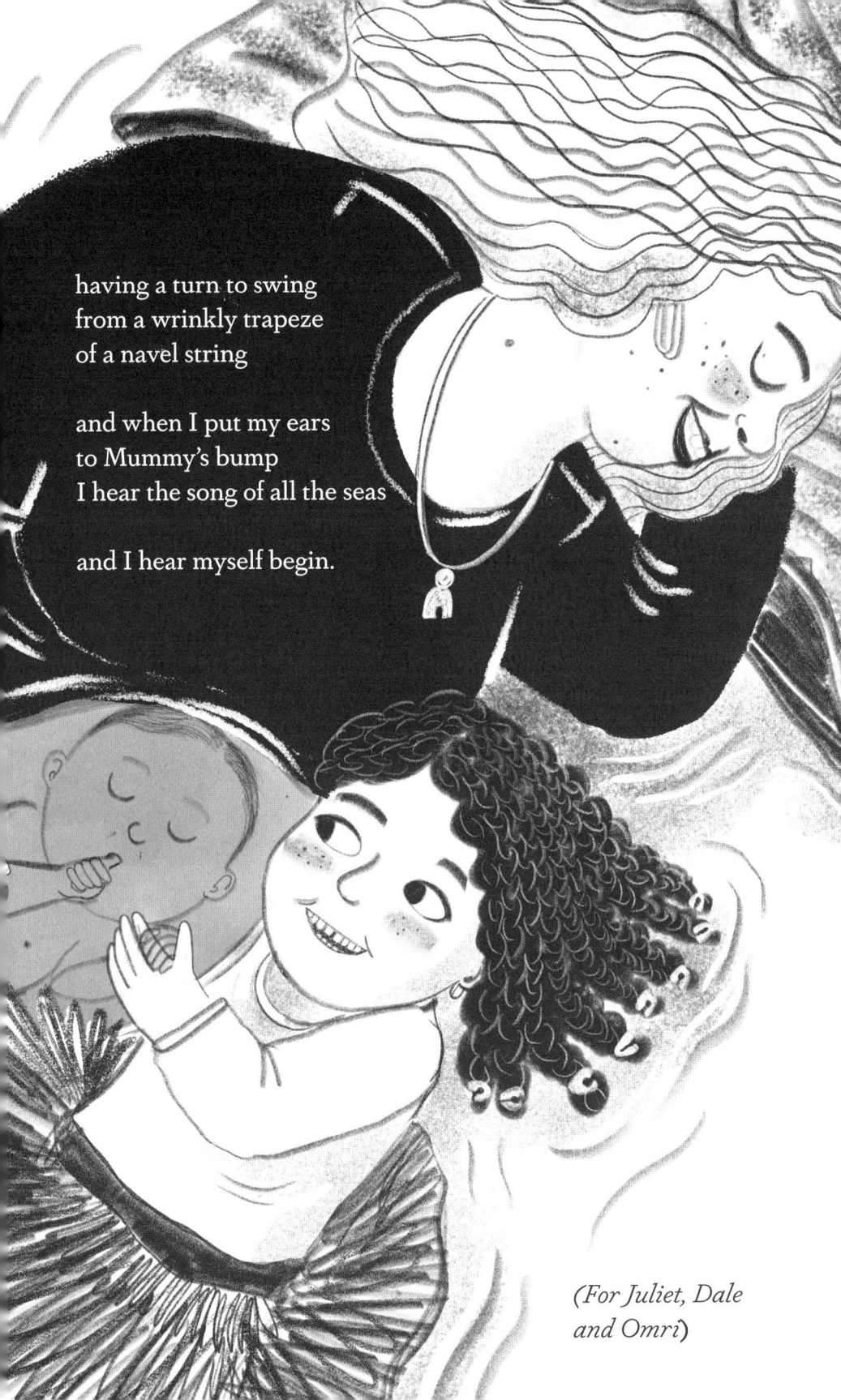

having a turn to swing
from a wrinkly trapeze
of a navel string

and when I put my ears
to Mummy's bump
I hear the song of all the seas

and I hear myself begin.

(For Juliet, Dale and Omri)

Globe

Spins like a ball
Round like a ball

In your hand it turns
And a whole world turns

Mountains rivers
forests lakes oceans

all one great swirl
of maps in motion

Spin it and spin it
till all countries orbit

in a merry-go-round
and everywhere gets a turn

to be upside down.

This Boomerang Will Keep its Word

You threw me from Down Under
all the way to Over Yonder

Suddenly wood grew wings
and I was flying with the wind

Once I was part of a tree
you brought out the bird in me

To your hand I will return
as bird to wood and wood to bird

This boomerang will keep its word
if you promise me one thing

Throw me once more to the wind
O throw me once more to the wind.

From

Points of View of Professor Peekaboo

SOMETIMES I GET THE IDEA for a title for a possible book of poems. The only thing is, I haven't written any of the poems as yet! *Professor Peekaboo* had a sound that appealed to me, because the word peekaboo made me think of a curious and even nosy person.

Probing into the mysteries of life, here is a professor who some would call wacky, zany, quirky, eccentric, maybe even mad in the best possible sense! But there is a side to him that is politically conscious and, from his peeking into the little things of life, he is enchanted by words.

For starters, he is a multi-linguist - he is fluent in many languages. He can communicate with pigs, because he speaks oink, he understands the meanings behind moo, and the language known as bleet (which, of course he mastered!) gives him the chance to communicate with his four-legged friends.

Once I'd entered the mind-space of this funny-serious professor, the poems began to happen. Inspiration came, as poems do, from familiar things, but being Professor Peekaboo, his views are oddly pitched.

You will see that I have not named the poems because I wanted you, the reader, to feel involved - to enter, as I did, the mind space of this professor. I felt naming the poems would get in the way of his fluid imagination.

It excites me to think that as you read these poems, you might also become part of that quirky mind, the mind of Professor Peekaboo. If you read this book on a Monday, curled up in bed or lounging on your sofa, spare a thought for the fact that Professor Peekaboo calls Monday Moonday, Tuesday Tubeday, Wednesday Webday and of course, Thursday is Thunderday, in honour of Thor.

Now who is this Thor? Professor Peekaboo with his passion for language and mythology is very much aware that the Norse God Thor gave his name to Thursday - not a bad day for a Norse God to put to rest his mythological hammer and chill out, looking forward to a long weekend and possible lie in!

John

I've studied a dog's bow-wow
and an owl's tu-wit-tu-wu

Recorded a cat's meow-meow
and a cock's cockle-doodle-doo.

Scribbled notes on a pig's oink-oink
and a cow's moo-moo

But how I long to know
sighed Professor Peekaboo

the extinct voice of one Dodo.

One sock green
one sock blue
to match each
odd-coloured shoe.

No. I'm not being trendy,
says Professor Peekaboo.
Only teaching my feet
to be environmentally friendly.

One foot for grass
one foot for sky.
Yes to things that crawl
yes to things that fly.

Walking in balance
between nature's gifts
So what if I dance
with socks and shoes mixed.

Green issues
are not to be treated lightly.
And quite rightly.

Or so Professor Peekaboo concluded
as he ponders forests denuded
and fish in rivers oil-slick-doomed
and air all laden with fumes.

So from his bed, he made a leap
and sat upon his compost heap.

It's such fun
to say tun-tun
the Chinook
word for heart

I often do
says Peekaboo
and roll my tongue
around the u

So let's get down
to the tun-tun
of the matter

Love someone
from the bottom
of your tun-tun

Distance makes
the tun-tun
grow fonder

Home is where
the tun-tun lies
Cross my tun-tun
and hope to die

O for a good
tun-tun
to tun-tun
conversation

Listen
to the throb
of your tun-tun

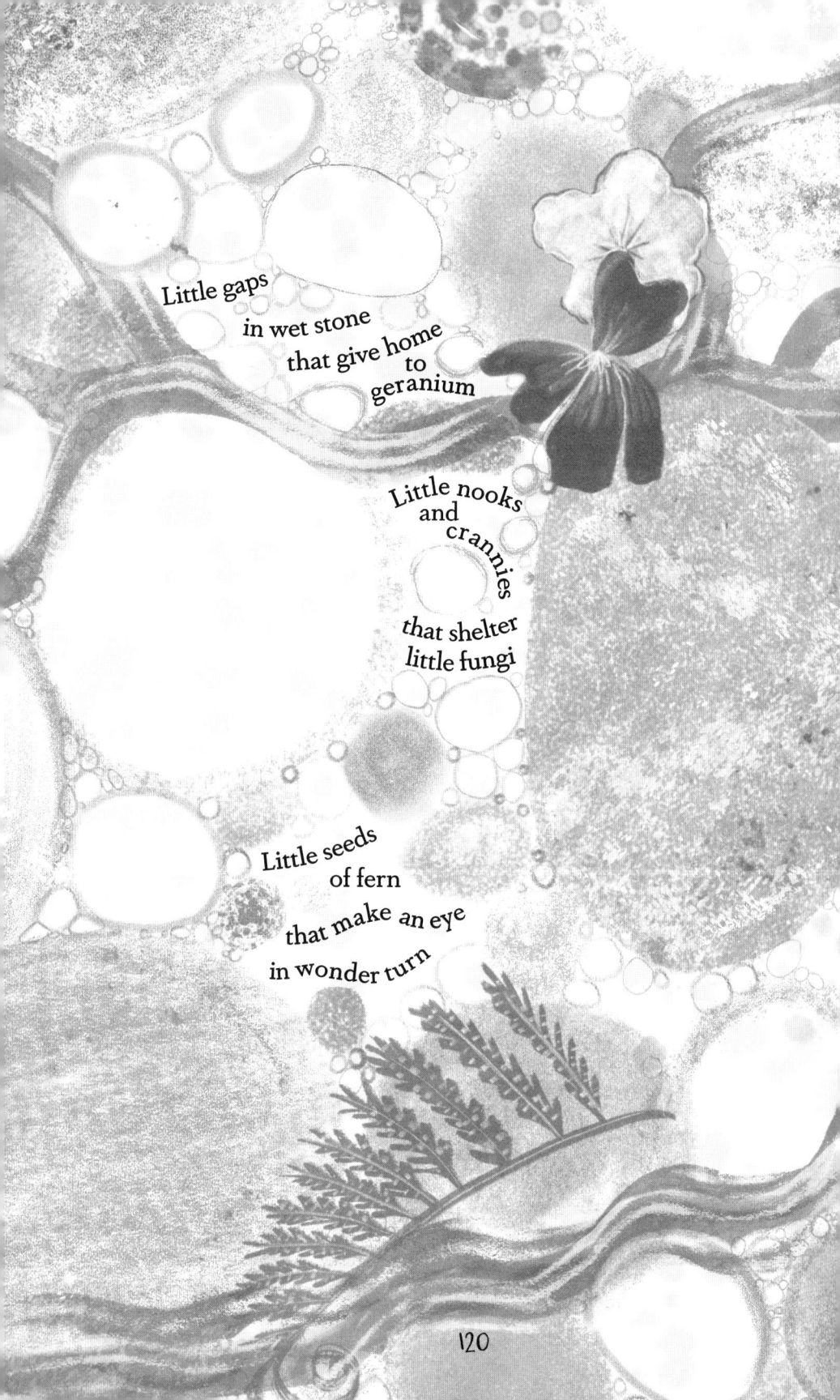

Little gaps
in wet stone
that give home
to
geranium

Little nooks
and
crannies
that shelter
little fungi

Little seeds
of fern
that make an eye
in wonder turn

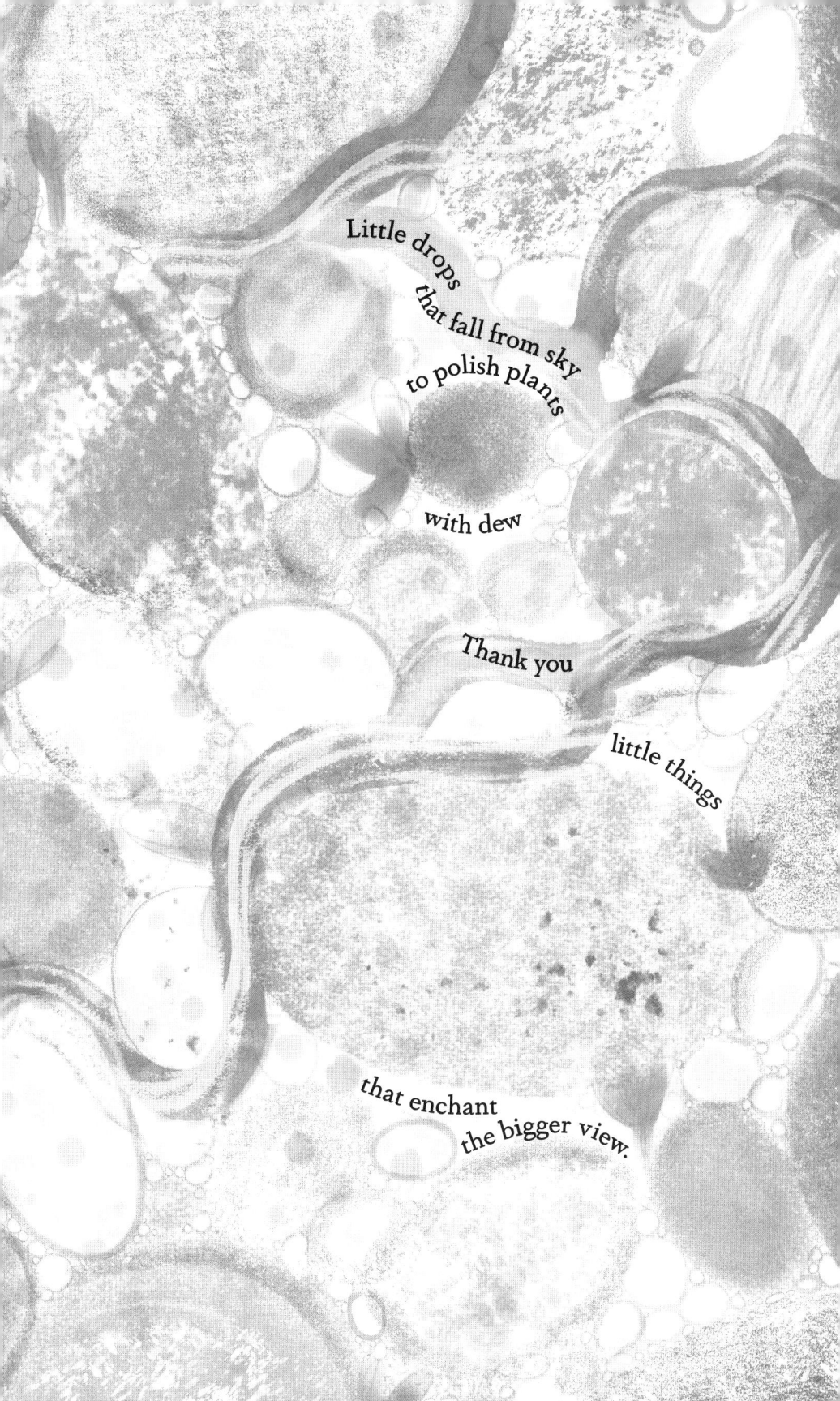

Little drops
that fall from sky
to polish plants

with dew

Thank you

little things

that enchant
the bigger view.

Why have two of Peekaboo
when one of Peekaboo would do?

No, thank you, I'll stay un-cloned.
Housed in singular flesh and bone.

But then again on second thoughts.
But then again on second thoughts.

Peekaboo one and Peekaboo two
could borrow each other's shoes

And argue on the telephone
about who's got whose chromosomes.

The black keys
always intrigued
Professor Peekaboo
who felt they were the clue
to the piano's mysteries.

You won't get far,
his music teacher advises.
You'll never be a Mozart
by leaving the white keys
to their own devices.

But Professor Peekaboo
even then a precocious child -
told his teacher with a smile.
Something tells me I have the knack
to compose Rhapsody in Black.

And true, said little Peekaboo,
there's a duet that I do
when a ghost comes out at night
and sits beside me on the stool.
This way I orbit black and white

and learn the key of midnight blue.

They stand to attention
for the wind's inspection

They take orders from the sun
and also obey the rain

They salute the skyline
and rustle their green bayonets

They often close ranks
but have no army tanks

They are only trees
as I am only Peekaboo

and their uniform is peace.

Oil slick, oil slick,
the sea is sick,
send for the doctor
quick-quick-quick.

Tell the siren-fish
to sound its alarm
Tell the drum-fish
to toll its drum

Ask what ails thee, Sea?

But no whales hum
No dolphins click

O what have we done?

MOONDAY
TUBEDAY
WEBDAY
THUNDERDAY
FRY-UPDAY
SATURNDAY
SAUNADAY

A relaxing end
to a busy week
says Peekaboo
MOONDAY will soon
be here again.

John Agard is one of the best loved and most distinguished poets of our time. He was born in Guyana and moved to Britain in 1977. He has published more than 50 poetry collections for both children and adults and has won many awards. He is a Fellow of the Royal Society of Literature. He was awarded the Queen's Gold Medal for Poetry in 2012 and received the BookTrust Lifetime Achievement Award in 2021. His poetry is on the GCSE English syllabus and he has toured widely with the GCSE Poetry Live show. He is married to fellow-poet Grace Nichols, and they live in Lewes, West Sussex.

Shirley Hottier was winner of the FAB illustration award in 2021. She is French and graduated in Paris with a degree in architecture. As an illustrator she has a passion for promoting diversity, drawing on her own family tradition of multiple cultures to create warm and lively scenes and characters. She is the illustrator of Patrick and the Not So Perfect Party. The Poetry World of John Agard is her first illustrated poetry collection. She lives in Edinburgh.